Chapter 1

The Detective

Many years ago, there was a magical woman called Danbrann who lived on a mountain, one day she decided that she didn't like being alone, so she climbed down the mountain to a little village and gave everyone who lived there a wonderful gift and they lived happily ever after until one day she disappeared without a trace.

Two weeks ago, in the slums of Sakkacity a stoic detective was drinking a cup of black coffee. It was his fourth one this evening, but it kept his hands steady, the last thing he needed right now was to be shaking in front of the witness, and with the creeping chill of the late December breeze crawling in he needed the warmth it provided. He wasn't exactly warmed to the soul by his present company, a crying neighbour, the jaded police officers, and a blood-stained corpse.

Donald Grail was a tall broad-shouldered man with short black hair, tired eyes, and slightly uneven stubble on his face. He had been described by many of his previous clients as 'standoffish' or 'impossible to read' but he considered these to be compliments, after all, no one would hire a private detective who would break at seeing a dead body, speaking of which, he knelt down next to the one he had been contracted to investigate, a young man, maybe mid-twenties, long blonde hair, glistening blue eyes that looked too filled with life to belong to a corpse, and fair skin still glowing with youth, a stark contrast from the stone-faced detective that stood above him. If it wasn't for the multiple knife wounds in his chest Grail probably would have made a point to complain about the fact that some people had their whole lives ahead of them while he withered away from age.

As he remained lost in his thoughts the nearby police officers attempted to comfort the neighbour who had apparently seen a shadowy figure slip away into the night so she came to check on the young man who lived here only to find that he was already dead, as she started sobbing into the chest of one of the cops Grail finally came back down to earth only to see her display and rolled his eyes before turning to face the rest of the room.

"It's the middle of December, the streets are caked in Christmas lights, if there was someone else here, they wouldn't be able to use shadows as cover." He spoke sullenly as he glared at the woman.

"Are you accusing me?" The neighbour asked with a face landing somewhere between surprised and offended. "Why would I call the police if I did it?" She retorted with a slight quiver to her voice. Grail simply sighed before pointing to the open window that led out to a street where any number of people could walk by and witness whatever may be occurring within those walls.

"Better for you to be the only witness." The woman started to get angry and pushed herself off the cop to come face to face with Grail who, as usual, seemed completely unfazed by the new turn of events, remaining as cold as ever as he calmly spoke again. "A man dressed in exclusively expensive clothing living in an apartment with nothing of value in it?" he gestures to the cops to search the two apartments before heading for the exit. "And for the record, ma'am, when people cry there are usually tears."

He remarked as he stepped out of the door pulling his heavy coat closed to face the brisk winter air.

As he made his way back to his office a young officer caught up to him, a bubbly young woman with red hair tied tightly back into a bun and freckles dotted across her button-nosed face, after a brief moment of trying to get the timing right she matched pace with Grail and introduced herself.

"Hi there! I'm Penny, I'm training here before I get stationed in another town, nice to meet you!" She said in an unusually chipper tone for someone who lived in this city. Grail looked at her with a blank expression for a moment and then gave a slight nod in acknowledgment. "I hope you don't mind me asking, but I saw you solve that mystery, and I still don't fully understand the motive?" She looked up at Grail expectantly as she waited for his answer, being quite a bit shorter than him she had to make the extra effort to stretch just to make eye contact which was especially difficult while walking.

"The kid had money, she didn't, jealousy and desperation could turn anyone into a monster... even you." He explained, Penny stopped in her tracks for a moment of quiet contemplation as Grail continued walking undisturbed by her presence, or lack thereof, before she caught back up with him and matched pace once again, regaining her bubbly optimism.

"Well, it's a good thing we had you to help, right?" she asked hoping to get some semblance of positivity out of him, but he simply grunts.

"Hiring me was an oversight on her part, nothing more." He replied as he unlocked the door to the small room that he rents to take phone calls and keep his files, he took a seat at his desk and leaned back breathing a sigh of relief to be back in his comfort zone, but Penny followed him inside and stood at the opposite end of the room facing him.

"It doesn't really make much sense that she hired you though, considering the facts that she already called the police and didn't actually want the murder solved... Why did she do that? She didn't strike me as being unintelligent in any way." She said mostly thinking out loud but also hoping to see the amazing detective that she had heard so much about from her co-workers in action solving a real mystery. Penny had always loved detectives ever since she was a little kid, crime novels were the main reason she even joined the police force in the first place but found that most of what she did these days was paperwork or ruining someone's day with a parking ticket or something. Grail thought about what she had said for a minute and his eyes darted between his files and the phone.

"She didn't hire me, that wasn't her voice on the phone." He announced with a tone of realisation that resembled more emotion than he had displayed all night up to this point and this was not lost on Penny, she knew, and he knew, that this case just got much more interesting. Penny of course pressed further.

"If there was no one else involved in the case then who would've hired you? Surely any witnesses would turn to the police first." She reasoned, Grail opened his mouth to speak but was interrupted by the phone ringing, he picked it up and let it speak out loud, a soft-spoken woman's voice came through as the two listened intently.

"Good evening mister Grail, I would like to continue doing business with you, if you'd be so kind, the next part of your case will take you to the small village of Anfarwol, I'm sure you'll be able to find your way from there, I have the utmost faith in your abilities." And with that she hung up without so much as a word uttered from Grail or Penny. They kept their eyes on the phone momentarily before looking at each other as Penny's face lit up.

"I'm going to be stationed in Anfarwol! We can work together!" She excitedly proclaimed, but before she could get too hyped up over working on a real mystery Grail shut her down.

"I'm not going." His words caused Penny's heart to sink, and she made no effort to hide this in her facial expressions, he stood up before she could begin her protest and opened the door again, gesturing for her to leave, she hung her head in disappointment and complied, heading back to the police station.

Grail closed the door behind her and sighed, interacting with other people took a lot out of him and he really enjoyed the end of the day when he could be alone like this. He sat at his desk and looked toward his window, he couldn't see what was outside due to his insistence on keeping the blinds closed at all times, not that he was particularly interested in what was going on out there, the way he saw it if there was something out there worth his time someone would hire him to look into it, on the other hand, someone had just hired him to look into a small village after calling him to a painfully basic open and shut case that they really had no business getting involved in, everything about it was shaping up to be an interesting case and considering what he was paid for taking on this client last time it could also prove to be fairly profitable, so what was it about her request that didn't sit right with him? He felt as though his life was in danger just by letting her talk to him.

"Maybe I'm just going senile in my old age." He thought before grabbing a pack of cigarettes and heading outside to face the world again.

Chapter 2

The Client

Grail walked the icy streets of Sakkacity, cigarette in hand as he thought about his life, Penny seemed to hold him in such high regard but to his memory she's the first one who ever did. People had told him he was a good man for solving crimes in the past but if he was honest with himself, he only really did it because he was good at it. He never had a particularly strong sense of morality, and he wasn't too concerned about what happened to the people around him, but taking cases paid the bills and the more he did it the less he had to deal with other people.

Grail had lived in a city his whole life, never having much money so he was used to making his home in a small space, often times dark and damp but he never let the sadness get to him, he would help out wherever he could being raised by a single mother and finding friends hard to come by. He found himself getting consistently good grades as he made his way through school and achieved a law degree but still hated interacting with people and decided that the courtroom wasn't where he belonged, aside from that he didn't really feel like he needed the money so instead opted to open a private detective agency.

He had made his money through university by taking whatever minimum wage job he could get but his mother was more than happy to offer what little she had to get him through and make a better life for himself until she passed away in his final year. He had hoped to one day make enough money to pull her out of debt but with that dream gone he was content to simply exist in his own world.

He was snapped out of his thoughts when he came to a small diner near the train station, he stepped inside and ordered a black coffee before sitting in a booth and staring out the window. He had come to this diner countless times but had no rapport with any of the staff, he wasn't interested in what they were doing, and the managers didn't care about the employees, so they were constantly cycling out.

He watched the rainfall and thought about the case, that woman's actions didn't make as much sense to him as he let on around Penny. He had sometimes thought there was some sort of outside force that controlled people to murder, that certainly felt like the case for this recent one, but he pushed that thought out of his mind as fast as he let it in, he'd have to be insane to legitimately believe in any kind of magic.

As he finished his coffee, as if on cue, his phone started to ring, pulling him away from watching the rain. He thought it was bizarre since he never gave out his phone number and only really carried it to look up relevant information to cases. He lifted the phone to his ear and heard the soft-spoken woman's voice once again.

"There is a train departing in 20 minutes, I'd ensure I was on board if I were you." She said, skipping the pleasantries.

"I haven't decided if I'm going yet." Grail responded.

"Well, the next train is going to take a few days, better decide quick." She said and immediately hung up. Grail paid for the coffee and left the diner, then stood outside the train station watching the platform and saw Penny boarding a train, he turned around and went back to his office. Over the next few days, he would be bombarded with phone calls from the woman and although he ignored the vast majority of them, they were starting to wear him down. The final straw was when she called him at four in the morning and only uttered a single sentence.

"The neighbour was innocent." She whispered and then hung up. Grail was furious, he packed his things and grabbed his coat, he was going to find out who this woman was and kill her. He headed out into the cold night air and made his way to the train station silently cursing himself out for admitting defeat with his actions.

Chapter 3

The Crime Scene

Grail headed toward the train station. The woman at the ticket stand smiled at him and spoke with a cheery disposition that slightly annoyed Grail. He never understood people who pretended to like their job, especially when they had to deal with someone like him. Grail understood that he was difficult, he was perceptive enough to notice that almost no one could hold a conversation with him, but he liked it better that way, people had a habit of getting in the way and he really didn't need the distraction.

He bought a black coffee at the cafe on the platform and sat down to wait for his train. As he waited he watched the various commuters going about their own lives, there was a man in a suit running to catch a train that was already departing with his shirt slightly untucked and tie loosened from running, a group of teenagers loitering on the platform laughing and chattering amongst themselves, a family being led down the platform by an angry mother who looked sleep deprived and ready to burst from having to deal with her kids. Grail leaned back into the bench and sipped his coffee, at least he didn't have a life, they seemed stressful.

He finished his drink just as his train screeched to a halt in the station, he stood up and threw the paper cup toward the bin, but it bounced off the rim and landed on the floor, he ignored it and kept walking onto the train before taking a seat next to the window and looking out at the Sakkacity sign. He had only left the city a few times since moving in all those years ago and it was usually to go to another city, not some tiny village in the middle of nowhere that he had never heard of.

He took a deep breath trying not to think about how far out of his element he's going to be. He took a moment to remind himself why he was doing this, he had managed to get himself interested and invested in a case for the first time in years, and he also needed to make next month's rent. He felt a slight jolt of movement as the wheels began turning and the Sakkacity sign slid out of view.

His eyes scanned the train car as he made a note of the other passengers, most seemed to be fairly ordinary people, nothing particularly striking about them, but one in particular caught his eye. One of the passengers had their head down and was wearing an oversized grey hoodie.

Everything about their body language made it seem like they were trying to hide their face from the other passengers, but why? Grail kept his eyes on this person throughout the rest of the train ride, switching between keeping tabs on their movement (or lack thereof) and staring out the window watching as he was carried away into the unknown.

As the train pulled to his stop, he got up ready to put the mysterious stranger out of his mind but then they stood up too and headed out onto the platform as Grail cautiously followed. The village he was headed toward didn't actually have a train station so he would have to walk the rest of the way and so left the city after stopping at the train reception to double check the directions but he was slightly off put by the clerks visible discomfort about the village, they seemed slightly uneasy about their own lack of information, he thought about that interaction a lot wondering what exactly was wrong with this village.

The road to the village was long and barren, it felt like it would never end as Grail trudged along occasionally turning back to check if there were any cars coming that he could hitchhike from, but the trail seemed completely lifeless. There were several points where he considered that this village didn't even really exist, but he had to believe because at this point turning around and going back seemed like way more effort than it was worth.

As he made his way along the path he found himself getting exhausted much faster than he thought he would, which was unusual for him since it wasn't like he was out of shape, he had spent plenty of time walking around Sakkacity and shouldn't be so worn out just walking in a straight line, Maybe this was why no one knew anything about this village, no one could make the journey, but he was being paid for it so he kept going.

Finally, he reached his destination, he saw the village of Anfarwol coming up on the horizon and quickened his pace, all he wanted to do was get a drink and take a nap, all he had to do was get to the end of the road. As he approached the entrance to the village, he noticed a small crowd gathered seemingly welcoming someone home.

He approached the crowd and saw the person they were welcoming was the hooded person from the train, they must have found an easier way here when they separated, and Grail checked the directions at the reception. No one seemed to notice Grail's arrival, and no one paid him any mind as the person removed their hood and Grail's world view was shattered in an instant.

Chapter 4

The Sheriff

Grail stood in the lift in the hotel trying to calm himself down as the floors slowly passed by, he watched the lights on the buttons blink higher and higher until he reached his floor. He took one more deep breath and tried to clear his mind as the doors opened but as he stepped out, he came face to face with a pink haired woman in clown make-up and brightly coloured clothing.

"The lift is out of service, please make your way to the stairs at the other end of this corridor." She informed him in a lively tone, twirling as she pointed down the hallway, Grail nodded and followed her direction but noted how strange of a gimmick it was, especially considering that no one in the lobby was dressed like that. He turned back to her, but she was gone. He was concerned and confused for a moment but put it out of his mind and continued down the corridor. As he walked, he noticed someone standing in the middle of the hall, he got closer approaching cautiously until he recognised the red hair and realised, he was looking at Penny from Sakkacity.

"Penny? What are you doing here?" he asked as he got closer to her. She didn't respond however, just stared into the distance looking away from him. He raised his hand and tapped her on the shoulder causing her to whip around and lock eyes with him. Only she didn't look like herself, her skin seemed to hang loosely off her body, and it almost felt like she was decomposing. He took a few steps back out of shock and opened his mouth to speak but was stopped by Penny starting to fall face first but sticking out her leg in front of her and catching herself to break into a sprint toward him, he turned around and started to run away from her.

He made it back to the lift and frantically tapped the button to call it back to his floor, he looked back and saw Penny charging towards him as she stumbled and crashed into the walls as she got closer and closer. The lift doors finally opened, and Grail ran in and started tapping the button for the ground floor, the doors slowly closed as he could see Penny rapidly approaching.

The door closed as she crashed into it and a mysterious black ooze started seeping through the crack in the door, Grail stood back and the ooze hit the floor and started spreading, he was unable to avoid it as it filled the entire floor and started rising, he tried to keep away from it as much as he could, but the lift was starting to fill completely with the ooze. As the blackness reached his neck, he lifted his face upwards to try and get as much air as possible before being submerged but was only able to last a few seconds before the darkness consumed him.

Grail woke up in a cold sweat, he looked around and saw the clock on the bedside table of the inn read 4:48 am, his eyes started darting around the room as he suddenly began remembering the night before. This village was too small to even have a hotel, he was staying at an inn on the floor above a pub, he hadn't seen Penny since she boarded the train, and there was really no explanation for that clown.

He stood up, had a shower and got dressed before heading back down to the pub, he saw Veronica the landlady look up at him as if relieved to see him walking around okay and waving to him, he tiredly waved back before heading out the door. Veronica was a tall intimidating woman with chin length brown hair who wore form fitting black t-shirts to show off the muscles she gained presumably from keeping the various drunk villagers in check, but she was able to shed that rough persona on the rare occasion when a new face would roll into town (at least long enough to sell them a room upstairs). Sat across from her at the bar was an old man with a long white beard holding a pint and keeping his head down, he did not acknowledge Grail as he left despite always being at the bar and seeing all the comings and goings.

Grail stepped outside and shielded his eyes from the sun, taking a moment to adjust to the harsh lighting. He looked around the village, his eyes stopping at the windows of each store as he considered where to start investigating. His main concern at the moment was that he didn't know what exactly he was doing there, and he was still missing a chunk of memory between arriving in town and buying a room at the inn. His thoughts were interrupted by the growling of his stomach so he decided that his investigation should begin in the cafe with breakfast.

"Welcome!" The owner, Maurice, called out enthusiastically almost immediately as Grail came through the door. People around him seemed to be getting almost invasively friendly recently which was a trend he hoped would die out quickly. "Hope you're feeling better today, friend, we were all pretty worried when you collapsed last night." The cafe owner continued. So, he collapsed then, that would explain the gap in his memory, and this guy seemed like he could be a good source of information.

"Good morning, my name is inspector Grail, I don't suppose you could answer a few questions for me?" He cut right to the point, not even waiting for a response before asking "What exactly happened to me last night? Do you know what caused me to lose consciousness and how I made it to the inn?"

"Bit of memory loss there, friend?" Maurice continued calling him friend despite having met him thirty seconds ago. Well, it's not every day we get a real-life detective in our quiet little village, I'll gladly help you out! You arrived not long after our good pal Daniel, he'd been gone for a while, out on a journey to the big city, but once you saw his face you went all pale and blacked out on the spot, it was the new sheriff in town who helped you out in the end, said she knew you from someplace." Grail's eyes shot open at that last comment.

"Where could she have known me from?" Grail asked out loud, but he was mostly talking to himself, he didn't really expect an answer from Maurice since he didn't even know the guy but to his surprise he piped up.

"Why don't you ask her yourself?" he replied as he gestured to the entrance. Grail turned around and saw Penny walking in, his heart stopped as he had a sudden flashback to his nightmare, and he wondered how much of it was based on reality. As they made eye contact her face lit up and she ran up to him, being almost a foot shorter she had forgotten how much she had to crane her neck to speak to him.

"Hey you're okay! I thought you said you weren't taking the case? How come you're here passing out in the plaza?" she excitedly asked, not reading the irritated and slightly embarrassed look on his face at the repeated mentions of him passing out last night.

"Circumstances changed, I felt like I should be here." He answered deliberately staying vague not wanting to admit he was mostly here because he didn't want the client to keep phoning him. "Anyway, why are you here?" He diverted the conversation away from himself.

"I told you before, I got transferred here after I finished my training." She reminded him about the conversation they had back in Sakkacity. "So, if you're solving a mystery here, I guess that means we'll be working together after all!" Her enthusiasm was palpable, and all Grail could do by way of a response was sigh in defeat.

Chapter 5

The Suspects

Grail and Penny sat together in the cafe eating breakfast as Penny ran through the people of interest in the town. There was of course Veronica the bartender, Cliff the old man who spent all his time at the pub, and Maurice the portly baker with the extravagant curly moustache but there was also Abigail the mayor who was a quiet and reclusive woman mostly elected for being well organised and good with paperwork, there was Graham the tailor who basically outfitted the entire village considering the miniscule population, there was Edith a kind elderly woman who lived with her grandchildren Jackson and Jasmine whose parents were a mystery and they didn't like talking about it, and finally there was Daniel, the man in a grey hoodie who arrived just before Grail, of course there were more people in the town but those were the ones Penny was most familiar with.

Grail suggested that they speak with each of them so he can gain some kind of idea on why he's even here. He had been in the dark too long now and it was starting to frustrate him, he needed a lead as soon as possible. Penny agreed and left her breakfast mostly uneaten on the table as she dragged Grail out the door and down the street to the first stop on their little tour of the village where they would meet the tailor.

Graham was a tall cleanly shaven man in a well fitted suit who carried himself with perfect posture, he would have been slightly shorter than

Grail if not for Grail's habit of slouching which allowed Graham to stand slightly taller, his hair seemed to be the only part of himself that wasn't perfectly presented, instead it was practically tossed back out of his face to allow him to focus on his work.

As Penny walked into the almost neurotically well organised store, she was greeted with a friendly smile that quickly turned to confusion as Grail followed close behind.

"Good morning, sir, is there anything I can assist you with today?" Graham asked with an elegant and soft-spoken voice that was almost the direct antithesis of Grail's harsh and gravelly one. Grail quickly looked the man over and then began silently inspecting the shop. It seemed fairly basic, there were mirrors and a stand for measuring, clothing racks filled with wares of various sizes and a room at the back where Graham could work on specially commissioned outfits. Graham turned his attention to Penny instead.

"He's not the biggest people person but he's here on a case and needs to meet the townsfolk."

She quickly explained hoping to avoid Graham getting upset at Grail's dismissive attitude. Grail finally approached him and glared at him as if attempting to see through his skull into his thoughts.

"Have you noticed any suspicious activity from anyone in town?" Grail asked bluntly, not breaking eye contact or even blinking as he questioned the increasingly frightened shop owner.

"N-no sir, you're the most curious character we've had around here in quite some time." He nervously answered trying to stay honest but deep down worrying that he might have said something to offend the large intimidating man in front of him.

Grail took no notice of it and instead backed off from the man and thanked him for his time before shaking his hand and walking out of the shop leaving Penny to apologise on his behalf before following him out into the street.

"You could have been a bit more polite in there, you know." She suggested slightly infuriate

"What wasn't polite about that? I barely talked to the guy." Grail asked nonchalantly as he continued walking.

"How are you so bad at socialising? I thought with all the suspects and witnesses that detectives would have to talk to people all the time." She observed while trying to keep pace with Grail who had seen Edith on a bench in a park and was making his way over fairly quickly. "Just let me do the talking this time" she said as she stepped in front of him.

Grail was happy to let her take the lead in conversation, she was right of course that his job did require more interaction than he was usually comfortable with, certainly more than he thought it would, but he found that with practice he became quite good at ignoring people without looking unprofessional, but that was when he was working alone and before he had that strange nightmare that was still weighing on his mind.

"Excuse me ma'am but could we take a moment of your time to ask you some questions? You're not in trouble or anything, we just want to know

if you've seen anyone acting unusual lately?"
Penny asked Edith with a very calming tone that
pulled Grail out of his own head and back to the
matter at hand.

Edith was a frail looking woman with white hair
down to her shoulders, she remained sitting as
she spoke, and Grail assumed by the walking
stick that lay propped up on the bench beside her
that standing could prove to be a difficult task
for her. Her answers were basic and revealed no
new information, so Grail let his eyes wander
around the park until he saw two children, a boy
and a girl, standing either side of a tree growing
next to a lake, they stared back at Grail with
emotionless expressions which he found to be
incredibly off-putting.

Finding nothing of value from continuing this
conversation the pair moved on, this time
heading toward a large house at the top of a hill
in the far side of the village, as they made their
way up the stairs Grail was distracted by the
intricate carvings in the stone pillars that lead to
an ornate door at the entrance of the house but
also noticed the vines wrapping around the
building and overgrown path suggesting that the

owner of the house didn't pay much attention to exterior maintenance, he remembered the earlier comments that Abigail the mayor was fairly reserved but was starting to feel like she was more of a total recluse.

His train of thought was once again interrupted by Penny as she rang the doorbell and took a few steps back to greet the person approaching the door while Grail stood a few steps back willing to let her do most of the talking again since she seemed to have developed a good relationship with the villagers in the short time she had been here, which wasn't too surprising considering her personality.

Grail thought about how Penny had already gotten to know all the people of interest in the village and how she had managed to talk her way into working on a case with him which is something he had exclusively done alone since the start but fact finding was definitely easier with her around and the more he thought about it the more it seemed like a good idea to keep her around, but he knew he was too stubborn for that, he wouldn't even know how to go about offering her the job.

Grail suddenly noticed that the door had been opened just a crack and a pair of green eyes were peeking through the gap watching them from being a pair of thickly rimmed glasses, Penny cheerfully greeted her and introduced Grail to whom she just looked at seemingly frightened of him.

"You know, he doesn't really like talking either, but someone's called him here to investigate some things and we're trying to find out why, do you think you can help?" Penny asked with an encouraging inflection, Abigail once again said nothing but his time she opened the door and gestured for them to follow, as she made a b-line to a room further down the hall Grail noticed the way she dressed seemed unusual for a mayor, she wore a simple t-shirt and plaid skirt with no shoes or socks, presumably because she had no intentions of leaving the house but her hair seemed particularly well maintained cut evenly at chin length it had a slight shimmer and bounced as she made her way to a desk where she produced a stack of papers that contained details of an upcoming festival that the village puts on every year.

"This is the only noteworthy thing I can think of, the village is pretty consistently quiet." She said as she handed the information to Penny, Grail froze upon hearing her voice for the first time. It was soft and quiet with a slight nervous shakiness to it but it was unmistakably the woman on the phone, the one who had hired him in the first place.

"It was you, why did you call me here if there was nothing wrong?" He demanded to know, thinking it best to address this immediately but the baffled look she gave in response made him slightly regret that move.

"You think she's the one who hired you?" Penny questioned trying to make sense of the situation, but Grail and Abigail just stared each other down as if they were conducting a psychic battle. This continued for only a few more seconds before Grail turned to leave forcing Penny to quickly apologise to Abigail and try to catch up to Grail on the way out once again.

"Mr Grail? I don't understand, why would she hire you to investigate something, not tell you what it is, then pretend she didn't?" She was now starting to see why Grail was getting frustrated over not having all the details earlier.

"Because there's something she wants to keep a secret, something's going to be revealed at that festival and I need to stop it before it does… and I'll need your help."

Chapter 6

The Victim

Grail awoke in a field, the sky was pitch black and he could only see a few feet in each direction, he rose to his feet and squinted trying to make out any objects around him but all he could see was darkness and the grass beneath his feet, so he walked forward a few steps. Unsure of exactly where he was or where he was going, he walked hesitantly, taking multiple breaks to try and get a feel of his surroundings until he heard the shaky voice of a frightened young girl crying out from the darkness.

With a clear destination in mind, he hit the ground running in the direction of the voice, after about a minute of running he saw the child emerge from the black abyss that surrounded them. Grail slowed down and approached her slowly, kneeling to come face to face with her. The girl looked at him with a blank expression, heavily contrasting the fearful tone in her voice. She was a short girl with large round green eyes and pink hair tied into pigtails and she wore a pink raincoat with a floral pattern embroidered onto the side.

Grail went to speak but before he had a chance, she raised her arm and pointed behind him, he followed her gaze and his eyes landed on a giant merry-go-round as tall as one of the skyscrapers in Sakkacity. He walked up to it and climbed onto the base but couldn't make it up to one of the horses.

The girl stood in place and watched him look around the enormous structure, never changing expressions and never saying a word until Grail realised that he was wasting his time examining the structure and made his way back to the girl before cautiously offering his hand, but she turned and ran in the opposite direction.

Grail wondered if she was afraid of him or something else and so looked behind him only to be greeted by an eight-foot-tall shadow that slowly stumbled towards him. Grail stood up fully and turned to run after the girl but as he did, he felt his movement getting slower, each motion of his arms and legs felt like a struggle.

He looked down to his legs and noticed a string tied to each one as well as his wrists, he followed them with his eyes back to the shadow that was still slowly approaching him, but the strings extended further beyond it and as Grail looked back to their origins, he saw them in the hands of the clown he saw in his hotel dream. He stopped running and locked eyes with the clown as the shadow reached him and engulfed him in it's arms covering everything for him in darkness.

Grail woke up on the floor of his room in the inn having fallen off the bed at some point during the night. Taking a moment to rub the sleep from his eyes and attempting to crack his back to alleviate some of the pain he decided he would go to the cafe again for breakfast today. He greeted Cliff and Veronica on his way out again silently hoping that if this was to become his new routine it wouldn't be accompanied by the nightmares.

He sat at the cafe with a black coffee and once again was quickly joined by Penny who excitedly ordered a blueberry muffin and joined him still giddy over working on a real mystery for the first time. She had initially hoped to start working on it officially yesterday but talking to all the villagers seemed to really take a lot out of Grail and he pretty much just wanted to go straight to bed, it raised certain questions about how he had functioned in his life up until now, but Penny thought it best not to pry.

"So where do we start?" She began, grabbing a notepad and pen.

"We need to know exactly what this festival entails, who's going to be there, what times, any major events taking place." He explained.

"Well, I've been looking over the files that Abigail gave us and it looks like there's a big parade where everyone wears masks and costumes, that seems like the best time to strike but I'm not sure who would do anything wrong around here." She reasoned. Grail nodded in response before resting his head in his hands, he sat in silence for a minute before borrowing Penny's notepad and pen and writing down a list of suspects, being all the people, he had met in the village, and the mysterious Daniel who's face he only saw once and can't remember. Penny looked over the list and questioned whether he thought Edith, Abigail or Jackson and Jasmine were legitimate threats, but his response was very characteristically simple.

"I don't trust them." He shrugged. Penny narrowed her eyes at that comment before she turned her attention back to the list as she continued reading names until her eyes widened and she looked back at Grail in shock.

"I'm on this list? You don't trust me?" She asked offended, Grail sipped his coffee in response as he looked out the window trying to avoid Penny's death glare. While he watched the passers-by he suddenly froze and stared at the man in the grey hoodie as he walked past the window. Penny got confused by his sudden change in demeanour so followed his gaze out the window and saw Daniel slipping out of view just in time.

Penny, not having the same sick feeling in her stomach that Grail had, stood up and started pursuing Daniel as Grail came to his senses and followed close behind. As they stepped outside, they found the streets strangely more crowded than they were used to and they found it increasingly difficult to chase him as their paths kept getting blocked by civilians.

Daniel slipped into an alleyway and came out to a stone path on a field that he followed around a hill to a small cottage shaded by a large oak tree on the hill. He stepped inside while Penny and Grail slowed down and approached the cottage cautiously. Grail put his arm out and stopped Penny progressing as he stared intently at the cottage, she put a gentle hand on his shoulder and looked at him with a sympathetic yet determined look.

"Wait here… I'll need the backup." He said with a slight quiver to his voice.

"I know you don't trust me, but I can help!" Penny insisted but Grail stood firm, putting both hands on her shoulders and leaning down to look deep into her eyes.

"Something's wrong here, it never takes me this long to get on top of a case, I can trust you enough to be here if something goes wrong but it'll be no good with both of us in danger." Grail justified, with tears welling up in her eyes Penny gave a resigned sigh and nodded as Grail turned around to face the cottage and walked through the door.

Inside he saw a mostly empty room with a lit fireplace and a solitary chair in the centre upon which sat the man in the grey hoodie, presumably expecting Grail as he sat with the hood covering his face. Grail slowly approached and Daniel finally removed the hood, his long blonde hair flowed down to his shoulders, and he looked at Grail with his glistening blue eyes. Grail stood frozen in disbelief, it was the man from his previous case, the one who was killed by his neighbour. How was he here? Why was he here? What did he want with Grail?

Penny stood outside with bated breath as she waited for something to happen, some indication that she should act but everything was eerily silent, and the anxiety was stirring in her stomach. Suddenly the foundation started to shake, and she started to panic. She wondered if she should step in, but she didn't know what she would do if she did, she thought to herself that Grail would know but then second guessed herself since he seemed to be mostly improvising, the only reason she was following him was because he was doing the job she always wanted, she should be on equal footing with him at least.

With a new determination she started running toward the cottage but was too late, the entire building collapsed in front of her. Her face drained of all colour and she started moving the rubble as fast as she could to try to find Grail but there was too much, she kept trying for hours until she was too tired to continue and dejectedly walked home unsure of what to do from this point on, with the lead detective and the main suspect gone there weren't many leads to follow.

Unless she took Grail's list and pushed harder into the rest of the town, after all their first line of questioning was so rudimentary because they didn't know any details. Penny stepped into her house with a new purpose, she was going to find out what was happening and avenge Grail's death. Alone if she had to.

Chapter 7

The Investigation

Penny woke up the next day and went about her morning routine as normal. Her dream was uneventful and quickly fading from memory as she headed out to the cafe for breakfast, trying to push down the memory of what she had seen the previous night, before questioning the other suspects. Ideally, she would have liked to have gone to the police station and catch up on paperwork, but the village was usually so quiet that her job was mostly admin around here and that isn't quite what she had in mind when she became a police officer.

She once again started with Graham, walking into the shop and sitting on a bench reserved for guests to sit on while they wait for a family member or a friend to be fitted for some clothes.

She asked him about his plans for the festival to which he paused and made her promise not to tell anyone before leading her to a back room where he showed her an extravagant costume full of feathers and coloured patches ready for the festival.

"Who's this for?" she asked, but he remained silent and looked back and forth between her and the costume for a few seconds before shrugging his shoulders. She looked at him confused and then followed up by asking "How are you making clothes for someone if you don't know who they are?"

"They sent me the request along with the proper measurements and money" He explained as he grabbed the letter out of a well organised filing cabinet and handing it to Penny who compared the handwriting to that of the paperwork that Abigail gave her and just as she suspected it matched up perfectly, she seemed to have a real penchant for hiring people anonymously but what was the purpose behind the outfit? Grail was clearly here to stop someone ruining the festival, but this just looked like a costume, she decided that the only way to get the answers she was looking for was to question Abigail herself.

She walked along the overgrown garden again to speak to Abigail but this time when she knocked on the door, she didn't receive an answer, she waited for a few minutes knocking multiple times, but nobody came so she assumed that this must be one of the rare occasions when she wasn't home. She turned around to leave and saw Edith walking with Jackson and Jasmine, she followed after them and caught up just as they were turning into the cafe. She stopped Edith to ask if she knew where Abigail went.

"No, I haven't seen her in a while, not since they refurbished the pub, I'm afraid." She responded as the twins found a table nearby. Penny asked what the relevance of the refurbishment was so she told her that Abigail will sometimes show up to present new businesses that open but she held a specific interest in that one in particular for some reason. Penny figured it was as good a lead as any and so headed to the pub to ask some more questions.

What she hadn't anticipated was walking in on Veronica pacing back and forth behind the bar looking worried, her eyes darted up toward to door when Penny walked in and she frantically asked if she had seen Grail since he didn't return last night, Penny's heart dropped as she realised that having gone straight home to get a handle of her own feelings, she hadn't thought to tell anyone else that Grail was dead. If she was being honest with herself, she had been running on the assumption that nobody else in town knew him well enough to like him, but it stands to reason that the bartender would, considering her affinity for the quiet things in life she probably appreciated Grail's cold and distant attitude. Penny took a seat and explained what happened.

A couple of hours had passed when Penny thought it was okay to ask some questions, she didn't want to push too hard and risk upsetting her but she needed answers, she asked about the refurbishments and Veronica told her that Abigail helped her fund some renovations a while ago on the condition that she had access to a small room in the basement, although she wouldn't say what she would use it for.

Penny asked to see it so Veronica lead her downstairs to the cellar and past the kegs and bottles to a small room containing nothing but a chair, a desk and a green metal locker that stood in the back corner of the room, Penny approached it but Veronica told her that Abigail has the only key so she'd need permission, Penny sighed now being back to square one and so asked Veronica if she knew what Abigail was doing, She seemed confused and insisted that Abigail would be at home since nothing important is happening until the festival but when Penny told her that Abigail was unresponsive she got concerned and agreed to help Penny look for her.

After showing Cliff out they went back to Abigail's house but once again received no answer when they knocked so Veronica decided to wait there to see if she returned while Penny went to see Maurice and ask if he had seen anything. Maurice happily welcomed her in as she came through the door but looked confused as she leaned against the counter instead of ordering food and sitting in her usual spot, he raised an eyebrow and cocked his head to the side as if to ask what she was up to, so she jumped straight to the questions.

"Would you mind me asking when the last time you saw the mayor was?"

"Well, that would be back when the pub was refurbished." He answered

"And what do you think she does in the meantime?"

"Well, I suppose mostly paperwork, trade routes and such, that politics is a lot of admin work I figure."

Penny narrowed her eyes in thought for a moment, it seemed that nobody had any real idea of what she did all day and rarely ever saw her, but if she was working that hard so consistently how come nobody had ever heard of the village? She was clearly up to something, and Penny was going to find out what it was.

As she left to meet back up with Veronica what she hadn't noticed was Jackson and Jasmine watching her intently as she questioned Maurice and making a note of where she was heading next. She arrived at Abigail's house and Veronica informed her that although nobody had come by, she heard a loud crash from the upstairs of the house, pretty much confirming their suspicions that Abigail was in there but just ignoring them.

"I usually don't like doing this but I'm starting to worry about running out of time." Penny admitted as she began knocking the door a lot harder and yelling into the house, Veronica was slightly taken back by how loud the normally soft-spoken sheriff could get when she wanted. They waited for a few moments but once again received no answer.

"Well, I suppose it's time to play the police card" She sighed before kicking down the door and walking in while pulling out her badge. Veronica tentatively followed behind her as they looked around the ground floor for Abigail. They split up to check all the rooms as fast as possible but didn't find her, just as they were about to ascend the stairs, they heard an unfamiliar voice from the front entrance. They looked at each other before turning around and slowly made their way back to the foyer where they saw the twins standing side by side in the doorway, Jasmine spoke first.

"You've overreached, officer." She said calmly with a very subtle hint of aggression which unsettled the two women.

"You're here to keep the peace, you're causing a ruckus." Jackson added, taking a similar eerie tone.

"Listen kids, we've got important work to do. Why don't you go find your grandma?" Veronica responded, bending at the knees to be eye level with the children.

"She's not available at the moment." Jasmine responded, allowing a sadistic grin to form as she spoke.

"And we can't let you continue." Jackson finished with an unnerving chuckle. Penny and Veronica looked at each other baffled for a moment and then slowly started walking to the stairs again when suddenly the twins ran forward faster than the two women knew they were capable of and attacked them, Penny and

Veronica struggled to get a hold of the twins as they were not only small but incredibly fast making it almost impossible to catch them but eventually after the twins had already landed several hits, Veronica was able to hold down Jasmine, Jackson saw this and abandoned his assault on Penny to try and help his sister. As creepy as they were they obviously cared about each other at least to some degree, unfortunately for the twins, however, this gave Penny enough time to get away and, with Veronica's insistence that she can handle the twins, run upstairs to find Abigail.

As she ran around the second floor, she noticed a door that didn't seem to fit the layout of the ground floor. Walking through it she found a spiral staircase that seemed to run along the inside of a tower connected to the back of the house, the stairs led up to a circular room at the top of the tower but also led down under the house to a cave dug out to fill a large circular crypt with walls covered in runes and a stage in the centre that had a four foot tall stone chalice in the middle, but it was the person in the room that caused Penny's heart to sink. Standing over the chalice and pouring a mysterious red liquid into it was Grail.

Chapter 8

The Motive

The cottage collapsed around Grail and Daniel, the support beams narrowly missed them, but the ceiling was quickly following, it didn't have a chance to harm them however because the floor gave way and they landed in an underground tunnel. Daniel stood first and ran down the tunnel out of sight, Grail shakily stood but had to crouch as he was too tall to fully stand. The cottage rubble had blocked off the exit, so he had no choice but to follow.

The tunnel was narrow and uneven, Grail felt as though it had been dug recently and in a hurry, he wasn't quite sure what that implied but what he did know was that Daniel had some explaining to do. He quickened his pace to a jog, not fully able to run due to the restrictive space and uneven floors but that wouldn't hinder him for too long as the path came to an end and he found himself in a large circular crypt with runes covering the walls, Daniel was standing next to a chalice staring at Grail.

"Sorry to have roped you into all this Mr Grail but I doubt you would have come had I simply just asked." Daniel said, finally breaking his silence.

"If you're talking now, you can answer some questions." Grail interrupted with a twinge of irritation to his voice.

"Yes of course, my name is Daniel and all I want is to escape this village." He explained as he started walking around the room. "I've come close a few times, but I never survive very long once they find me, none of us do. Of course, most of the villagers are content to live their ordinary lives but they can only cope for so long before they snap like the rest of us."

"What the hell are you talking about?" Asked Grail, exhausted from all the theatrics and just wanting some straight answers.

"The people in this town don't die, Grail, we can't move on, we can't leave and if we try, they find us, kill us, and bring us back." He explained, Grail looked at him with a baffled gaze before turning around and silently leaving the way he came in. Daniel ran after him as he called out that he needed his help. Grail completely ignored him as he tried to dig out of the cottage rubble hearing the faint sounds of Penny panicking on the surface.

"Mr Grail, please, an immortal can't conduct the ritual, I've specifically chosen you to be my accolade. Now stop being so difficult and come back to the crypt." Daniel angrily said while tugging on the back of Grail's coat. Grail scowled at him before following him back and then investigated the stone chalice to see some broken crystal shards and plants piled up in the bowl, he looked back at Daniel with a disapproving gaze as he picked up a small ornate wooden box and brought it to Grail. Inside the box was a short ceremonial dagger which Daniel used to draw blood from his hand and pour it into the chalice.

The blood mixed with the other ingredients, and they started melting down into a red elixir, not quite blood but not entirely unlike it either.

Daniel reached into the box one more time and pulled out a small wooden cup which he filled with the elixir and gave to Grail who looked at him and cocked an eyebrow.

"There are three other crypts like this one hidden under various points of the village, I need you to pour this into each of the chalices." He said, looking expectantly at Grail.

"Okay first of all, why don't you just do it yourself? Second, what makes you think I'll help?" Grail asked, getting increasingly irritated by Daniel's complete inability to sense Grail's boundaries.

"Well, this crypt is slightly different to the others in that it was built by me, the others weren't, immortals can only enter the crypts they built. And I think you'll help me because I'm the lesser of the evils." He responded with a slight arrogant smirk. Grail took the cup and lid and asked how he was supposed to get out, so Daniel led him to the opposite side of the crypt where he opened a secret door that led to a staircase to the surface.

Upon reaching the top of the stairs Grail held his hand over his eyes to shield them from the sun while his eyes adjusted to the change in light. Daniel told him that he should stay hidden for now since Penny has most likely told people that he's dead before he went back down the stairs and the entrance to the staircase sealed behind him. Grail figured that was probably the best course of action while he figured out what he wanted to do.

He knew that Abigail was up to something and that it directly opposed Daniel's goals, perhaps she was the greater of the evils that he was talking about. He figured that if he could talk to Abigail then he could learn which of them he should trust and maybe he could find out what the elixirs and stone chalices actually do. At the very least Daniel seemed to be under the false impression that they were working together for now so that should stop him from doing anything too rash, but he also wanted to figure out why Daniel was so insistent that he had to be the one to help.

There was a lot to unpack but the first order of business was clearly drawing out Abigail without being noticed by the villagers. For now, he decided to try and ignore the supernatural elements at play and chalk it up to Daniel being insane… Surely there was a reason Grail had seen him dead a few days ago… Surely nobody could really come back to life… Grail needed some sleep. Badly.

Chapter 9

The Alibi

Grail found himself alone in a dark empty room, it was dark enough to where he couldn't quite tell where the floor ended, and the walls began. He looked around and noticed that on one of the far ends of the room there was a doorway with a small crack of light shining through onto the floor. He approached it and pushed against the door, but it didn't budge, He leant against it pushing it with his shoulder but once again made no progress. Stuck for ideas he tried knocking the door and to his surprise it creaked open. Opening inwards, it took a second to reveal that on the other side of the door awaited the woman in the clown make-up who remained silent and pointed behind her, inviting Grail to step out of the dark room.

He instead found himself at the top of a stairwell that led to a foyer and an ornate set of double doors presumably leading outside. He turned back around to look at the clown only to find that she had once again disappeared, so he instead turned his attention back to the stairs where he noticed the small girl from the merry-go-round in the field. The little girl looked like she was trying to get down the stairs but was having a hard time as she repeatedly began to take a step down but raised her foot back up seeming like she was afraid of committing to the journey.

Grail walked up to the little girl and just as before found himself not exchanging any words with her, just reaching out his hand and wordlessly offering his assistance. Unlike last time however, she wasn't hesitant and gladly took his hand as they started walking down the stairs together. They took it slowly moving one step at a time but as they progressed Grail could feel his throat closing up and his heart rate increasing, as if he was frightened of what he would find beyond the double doors. He wondered if the girl felt the same dread as they continued their descent.

Finally, they reached the bottom step and he started to head toward the large doors, but the girl held tightly onto his hand and didn't move, pulling him back to her. She locked eyes with him, and they stared at each other for a few seconds. He noticed that her pupils started to grow, he started getting concerned as they encompassed her entire eyes and as he tried to pull away from her the blackness grew beyond her face and covered everything consuming him once more.

Grail woke up under a tree and struggled to stand. He really needed to get a better night's rest if he was going to figure anything out. Coffee was out of the question since he couldn't get to the cafe without being seen but he could walk over the hill and through the woods that surrounded the village to get to Abigail's house. As he was trudging through the trees he noticed the lack of any kind of wildlife, it wasn't something that had jumped out to him immediately, but he started to realise that he hadn't seen any animals since he'd come to the village, and he started to wonder if it had something to do with the immortality that Daniel was talking about before.

He came to a wooden fence cutting off the forest from a garden, taking a small run up and vaulting over the fence, he saw the back of Abigail's house. Once again, the garden was overgrown and there were vines crawling up the walls but what really caught his attention was the tower at the centre back of the house that couldn't be seen from other angles. He made his way up to the house and found the back door locked, realising that he'll need to talk with Abigail anyway he decided that it was okay if she knew he was still alive and knocked the door. A few minutes passed with Grail knocking twice more when he heard the chain latch on the inside being shakily undone, followed by the door opening just a crack and Abigail's eyes peering through it.

"We need to talk." Said Grail making intense eye contact. Abigail, seemingly having figured out that Grail knows more than she thought, opened the door and let him in. She led him to her living room where they each sat on a separate sofa facing each other with a wooden coffee table separating them. They sat in silence for longer than most people would be comfortable with and then finally it was Grail to break the silence.

"I need to know why you hired me."

"By now you likely know the secret of this village, nobody dies here, not that we're invincible or anything, but we don't age and we always come back from ailments that would otherwise be fatal. Not everyone in town knows about it, however. We don't know the true source of this power but those of us with any control take great care to ensure that the power stays within this village, and that means convincing the villagers that it doesn't exist." She explained, suddenly becoming much more talkative than she's ever been and confirming that Daniel was actually telling the truth.

"Well, it's nice to finally get an explanation but you've avoided my question." Grail pressed further.

"Someone wants to take away the power. From all of us. It's not a new concept we've dealt with uprisings before but this one's avoided capture and made it out of the village more times than I care to admit. I hired you to stop them before they get the chance. To save the lives of everyone in the village." She told him with a dramatic stare.

"Why not just let them leave?" Grail asked.

"Could you imagine the calamity if people saw a corpse get up and walk around?! We can't let the outside world see that!" Abigail yelled. Suddenly there was a knock on the door and they both froze, a few minutes passed, and the door was knocked several more times in between but they both sat still and silent giving no indication that there was someone home.

Eventually they heard whoever it was give up and walk away so they both breathed a sigh of relief before Abigail gestured to the staircase and they both went upstairs, Grail spotted the doorway to the tower and asked her if it had any relevance, her eyes widened, and her breath stopped short for a second before she regained her composure and insisted it was nothing.

Abigail walked into her bedroom and pulled a box from under her bed identical to the one Daniel had used to fill the stone chalice. She put it on a vanity and opened it up to reveal a dagger and a cup exactly like the ones Daniel had but before she could do anything with it the phone on her bedside table began to ring. She walked over and picked it up when was greeted by the twins who told her that Penny was asking questions about her in the cafe and seemed close to finding out what was under the pub. Abigail thanked them quickly then hung up.

"Why are you keeping tabs on Penny?" Asked Grail, suddenly growing much more distrustful of the mayor.

"It's not often a mortal moves into town, you two are the only ones. Just need to make sure I can trust you." She responded with a clearly faked positive tone.

"Okay then, trust me. Tell me what's under the pub, tell me why you're afraid to bring up the tower." Grail asserted. Abigail went silent and glared at him, letting her eyes briefly dart down towards the dagger and back up to him. They both stared at each other for a few seconds mentally calculating their next move when they both at the same time began running. Abigail went for the dagger and Grail ran for the door to the tower. He crashed through the door and ran up the stairs to a small circular room then shut the door behind him as Abigail waited outside knowing that there were no other exits.

Grail wasn't sure how long he waited in there but with nothing of use in the room he knew he had no options beyond outlasting Abigail. It was only when he heard some knocking on the door again did, he come up with an escape plan, he realised that Abigail wasn't going to go greet them, so he climbed out the window and onto the roof of the house. He saw Penny leaving but still heard footsteps around the house.

He started walking to the front, but the roof wasn't built to withstand his weight and he was pretty heavy footed, so it broke beneath him and he fell through into Abigail's room. He sat up groaning from the pain but then realised that Abigail had left the box with the cup in there. He grabbed it and hid in the wardrobe until Abigail came running in to see what the noise was. Grail jumped her and after a scuffle knocked her unconscious and grabbed the dagger. He looked around the house for a while but decided the only place of note was the tower so went downstairs this time and found Abigail's crypt. He slowly entered and found her chalice empty, presumably she would have used it to create the same elixir that Daniel had made before.

Grail sat and contemplated for a few minutes about who he'd rather trust. Abigail was much more direct, giving him straight answers while Daniel had a habit of talking in circles. On the other hand, Daniel never chased him with a dagger. Finally, he rationalised his decision to himself by considering the other two chalices somewhere in the village. He could activate this one and see what it does, then make his decision from there. He stood up and walked to the chalice, opened the cup that Daniel had given to him and began pouring the elixir into it when suddenly he heard a gasp and turned to the entrance to see Penny's horrified expression.

Chapter 10

The Breakthrough

Penny and Grail stood staring at each other for a few moments before Penny screamed and demanded to know how he was still alive and what he was doing. He tried his best to explain but kept stuttering and tripping over his words as he attempted to recount all the bizarre things he'd seen and heard but she seemed somewhat hung up on the fact that he wasn't dead for some reason. She walked into the crypt and investigated the chalice to see what Grail was pouring in there.

"What does it do?" She asked apprehensively.

"That's what I'm trying to figure out." He answered.

"And then you were going to tell me why you're alive?" She asked, still clinging onto the hope that he was telling the truth outside of the cottage. When Grail admitted that he hadn't thought that far ahead she fully believed him, but she also believed him when he went on to say that he had no intention of hiding from her forever.

"Okay, fine. I forgive you, but don't you ever leave me in the dark like that again!" She shouted at him while punching his arm to punctuate every word in the last sentence. "We're equal partners in this whether you like it or not." Grail was surprised by her newfound assertiveness, but it was a welcome change from her overly soft personality from when they met.

Nothing seemed to happen in the crypt when Grail poured the elixir into the chalice, so they went back upstairs to see if it had any effect on the outside world, Penny started heading for the staircase to check on Veronica, but Grail went to Abigail's room, so Penny followed him asking what he was doing. He explained that he had left Abigail there but when they entered the room, they found her gone.

Panicked, Penny told Grail to follow her and get Veronica's help again but when they got downstairs, they saw that both she and the twins had disappeared as well. They were growing more concerned so left the house and explored the village only to find that everyone else was perfectly fine and just going about their normal lives.

They looked around as much as they could for Veronica but after a while Grail was ready to give up asking why Penny wanted to find her so bad in the first place, so she told him that she gave her a big lead, helped her find Grail, and fended off the twins. She was prepared to explain that the twins attacked them and had been working with Abigail in some way, but Grail brushed it off saying he knew they were too creepy to be normal kids right from the start. He instead directed the conversation to the supposed lead Veronica gave her, so Penny told him about the locker that only Abigail has access to. Grail pointed out that Abigail is now missing and nobody in town has noticed, meaning they have free reign of her house and could probably find the key relatively easily.

They both sprinted back to the house and started pulling out every draw, cupboard, and sofa cushion looking for any keys that could open the locker. They had searched most rooms in the house when they suddenly heard a knock at the door. They both looked at each other then across the destroyed house until their eyes landed on the door. Grail gestured to it with a tilt of his head and Penny slowly approached the door. She called out without opening it.

"Who is it?" She asked, doing her best to imitate Abigail's voice.

"Ms. Mayor? I brought back the key you asked me to hold onto, I know you told me to keep it until the detective left but Cliff said he went missing yesterday." The voice called back from the other side. It was clearly the key they were looking for, but they couldn't let him in, or he'd see the destroyed house, he'd see Grail, and he wouldn't see Abigail.

Penny pointed to the bathroom door indicating to Grail that he should hide while she opened the door. She opened it just enough that she could squeeze through while blocking the view into the house. On the other side of the door, she saw Graham holding a small key.

"Oh, hello Sheriff, what are you doing in the mayor's house?" He asked, narrowing his eyes with suspicion as he eyed the slightly frayed door frame from when Penny kicked it in.

"I'm working on a case, can't reveal details but I need to keep Abigail with me for a while, I can give her a message if you'd like?" She answered, hoping to steer the conversation away from Abigail and toward the key. Graham instead said it wasn't important, then he put the key in his pocket and walked away. Penny called out Grail to tell him that they're going to have to steal the key from the Tailor's shop. Grail groaned in frustration.

Within the hour Graham had made it back to his shop and was working on the costume some more when he heard a faint knock at the door, especially confusing since people typically just walked in, so he got up and opened the door but didn't see anyone. He looked around and saw a shadow against the wall leading down the side of his building down an alleyway, he followed it down and saw Grail who started telling him about everything that had happened but exaggerated the details and made it sound like the ravings of a madman.

Graham stood and listened in awe, completely unsure of what to make of this man who he thought was supposed to be a stoic detective. While Grail was distracting him Penny walked in through the front entrance and ran to the back room to look for the key, she knocked all the items off the desk and pulled files out of some cabinets looking for it making the place look significantly more disorganised, but she found the key and noticed that the costume had been adorned with crystal shards at some point.

As Penny left, the door swung closed and rang the bell at the entrance which piqued Graham's interest, so he walked back to the entrance and saw Penny running away. He went to go after her, but Grail started running in the opposite direction and in trying to chase both of them he lost them both. They rendezvoused at the pub and Penny led the way down to the room in the basement.

They entered the room and Grail made a note of how empty it was, like it had no real reason to exist. Penny suggested that whatever was in the locker would be the room's purpose as she unlocked it and opened the door to see that there was nothing actually in the locker. There was, however, a hole at the bottom that connected to a ladder which goes down into another cave. Grail went down first and found yet another crypt with yet another stone chalice in the centre. The two of them approached the chalice and found it empty which was somewhat relieving. Just as they began discussing who this crypt could belong to, they heard an unfamiliar voice at the entrance, they turned around slowly and saw Cliff standing inside the crypt.

"You've been busy." He remarked

"So now you decide to do something?" Asked Grail.

"Well, I'm afraid I didn't have much of a choice." Cliff said. Grail and Penny looked at him confused. "I'll happily explain myself now, though." He continued. "You see those chalices are used by immortals to create an elixir. You must build your own crypt to have access to one though and that opens you up as a target. You see if you can trick a mortal into pouring your elixir into someone else's chalice, whoever owns said chalice becomes your puppet. That was the case of Abigail, you're not the first detective she's hired and tried to trick but they usually go mad or die before they can turn against her like you did. She had control of almost all the chalices too, as you know the only ones left who know how to make one are the elders, consisting of Abigail, Daniel, Myself, Jackson and Jasmine. But now that Daniel has control of Abigail, her control over the twins and I have vanished." He exposited.

"Wow that's a lot to unpack all at once." Penny noted, taking a seat on the floor.

"Well, I've been a spy for long enough, taking notes on the comings and goings of the inn. You deserved a proper explanation." He added.

"So, if Abigail and Daniel are fighting over total power, what are you and the twins doing?" Grail asked, desperate to close this confusing case.

"The twins are a hateful pair, being cursed with immortality at such a young age, they want nothing more than the deaths of everyone in this village. As for me I just want to break this curse, this village is unnatural, and the fighting will never end if we don't release it." The old man explained. Penny jumped up and frantically interrupted.

"Wait but what about Veronica? I think the twins have her!" She pointed out getting slightly worked up over the thought of what they might do to her. The old man reached into his pocket and gave them a map of the village with four points marked on it signifying the locations of the four crypts. He told them that they'll need to remove their powers and to do that they'll need to create an elixir using mortal blood and pour it into each of the chalices. Penny asked how they create an elixir so Grail revealed the dagger and cup he stole from Abigail and told them that he watched Daniel make some and can recreate it.

Chapter 11

The Elixir

Grail headed back into the forest, knowing he was safe with the lack of any wildlife around he started looking around the shrubbery for the same plants he saw Daniel using when he made the elixir. As he dug through the many different kinds of plants, he realised that most of them looked a lot alike and wondered how people studied these things for a living. He ended up just basing his selections on the number of points each leaf had and making some educated guesses. He cut up his hand a bit on some of the nettles but managed to get everything he needed. He was about to make his way back to town but heard some unusual sounds in the distance. Knowing they couldn't just be animals he headed deeper into the woods to investigate.

He followed the muffled sounds and climbed over some bushes and through some trees. It took a few minutes to pinpoint the exact location of the sound but eventually he managed to track it to a seemingly unassuming tree in the middle of a small clearing in the woods. Knocking on the side of the trunk he found that the bark had been attached manually to a metal frame. He pulled it off and found a rusty door which he had to pry open with a stick.

Inside he saw that it didn't lead anywhere, it was just a hollow tube with Veronica sitting inside tied up, gagged, and surrounded by skeletons.

Grail untied her and she scrambled out as fast as she could to get away from the corpses.

"How did you get in there?" Grail asked.

"I just woke up there after Jackson and Jasmine knocked me out." She explained.

"Why would they go through the effort of locking you in there?"

"It takes a long time to create the elixir that can kill an immortal, they just needed me out of the way. Also, apparently, I'm immortal, they didn't care for the fact that I didn't want to join them after they told me that little detail."

"We've got a plan to remove everyone's immortality, it should put a stop to the fighting, you want in?" Grail suggested, knowing Penny would appreciate having Veronica around.

Veronica agreed that it was for the best, so Grail led the way back to Cliff's crypt. Meanwhile Penny hid in the alleyway by the tailor's shop awaiting an opportune moment when he would leave for long enough for her to dive in and grab the crystals that she had seen on the costume last time she was there, they seemed to fit the ones from Grail's description of Daniel's elixir. Although it seemed that her previous hijinks in his office have left him preoccupied with trying to reorganise everything while trying to stay on top of his normal workload, this was reflected in his appearance as he displayed a more dishevelled look than his usual prim and proper persona.

She didn't want to make life more difficult for him, but Daniel was an unknown element and shaping up to be a real threat on top of the twins who were already a serious problem and she needed those crystals if she was going to stop them, so she walked down the road and entered the shop through the front entrance.

She once again heard the little bell above the door ring as she entered and heard Graham in the back call out that he'll be there in just a second. When he walked into the front room and saw Penny his face dropped, and he went to escort her out while telling her that she's no longer welcome in his shop. Penny started protesting and insisting that there's a good reason. Graham sighed and stopped trying to push her out the door, he then stepped back and looked at her expectantly giving her the indication that she should elaborate.

"I need the crystals on that costume you were working on." She said quickly and quietly as if he would have blindly accepted anything she said if he didn't hear her clearly enough. Of course, what actually happened was that he immediately started trying to push her outside again. She had to resort to pushing him back, ducking under his arm, and running to grab the costume. She locked the door to the office behind her so he couldn't stop her. She shouted through the door how sorry she was and turned back to the costume.

With no time to remove the crystals with Graham threatening to kick the door down she had to grab the whole thing and climb out the window to avoid running into him again. As he saw her running down the street, already too far away for him to catch up she was profusely apologising. Within the next hour he had put a poster in his shop window announcing that she was no longer welcome within his establishment.

Back beneath the pub Penny sat on the chair with her head resting on the desk next to the costume lazily lumped onto it in the room with the locker. Grail walked in behind her during one of the rare occasions when he was smiling until he saw her looking depressed and his facial expression shifted to one of a concerned parental figure.

"What's wrong?" He asked. Without lifting her head and mostly mumbling into her arms she explained what happened and how she felt bad about repeatedly being a bulldozer in Graham's day but Grail simply smiled in response as he knew he had the perfect thing to make her feel better.

"Look who I found." He said coyly as he stepped to the side and let Veronica walk into view, Penny's face lit up and she jumped out of the chair to run up and hug Veronica telling her how worried she was when she vanished. Veronica comforted her and told her what she told Grail about the twins teaching her some of the immortal magic. Penny thanked Grail for saving her and decided she would stay upstairs with Veronica and gather information about the twins since Veronica couldn't enter the crypt, while Grail and Cliff used the ingredients gathered to create the elixir.

They had crushed up the crystals and mixed in the correct plants when Grail brandished the dagger and held it to his hand but hesitated, he looked to the old man and asked if this was really the best course of action. Cliff reminded him that he can back out at any time but if the power-hungry elders kept their powers, then they would only grow more and more powerful.

Grail lowered the knife and wanted Cliff to elaborate so he produced a book that details the story of Danbrann who an elder immortal was many years ago but was killed by her partner after she gained control over every other immortal. Danbrann had gained so much power that she was able to use the elixir to control mortals without the need for a chalice. She began her conquest on the village that lay below the mountain that they lived on, but she never made it further than that. After she died the inhabitants of the village that she had controlled were all granted immortality but most of them remained unaware and the ones that did know fought amongst themselves until there were only five left.

"Who was the partner? Who killed Danbrann?" Grail asked, already suspecting that he knew the answer.

"It was me. I knew then as I do now that this curse should not spread, and nobody should have that kind of power." Cliff confirmed, staring at the elixir ingredients as if to indicate that Grail would have to be the one to finish what he started all those years ago. With that Grail raised his hand once more and poured his blood into the chalice creating the elixir that would remove their immortality. It took effect on Cliff immediately as he grew tired and crumbled to the ground.

Grail panicked and picked him up to carry him back up the stairs where he saw Penny and Veronica catching each other up on all sides of the story. They both stopped talking and jumped up when they saw Cliff in his condition, then helped Grail carry him upstairs to a room in the inn to let him rest. The three of them looked at each other with a sense of nervous determination as the setting sun shone through the window ready for what the next day would bring.

Chapter 12

The Festival

Grail woke up from the first decent night's sleep he had since he arrived in the village, he headed downstairs to the pub and saw Veronica standing behind the bar, where she was most comfortable, and Penny sitting on a barstool with a glass of orange juice. Grail took a seat next to her and Veronica handed him a mug of black coffee that she had already prepared for him. The three of them sat in silence as they began to hear the sounds of music and celebration in the streets.

As they mentally prepared themselves for what was to come, Veronica stayed behind to keep an eye on the village as she opened the pub for business and the customers started rolling in. Penny and Grail donned some festival masks and disappeared into the crowd.

While he made his way through the crowds, trying not to draw too much attention to himself he noticed that some people had chosen to forego the masks in favour of painting their faces with clown make-up. He brushed it off as a coincidence at first, surely it had nothing to do with the dreams. He was maintaining his composure until he looked toward the cafe and sitting there in the same spot, he sat in every day to drink his coffee he saw her, the very same clown from his dreams. He felt his stomach drop and his heartbeat quicken as he began hyperventilating, he didn't know how this was possible, but he didn't care right now he just had to get away from all these people.

The only thing he could think of doing at that moment was heading to the cottage so he ran there as fast as he could, causing multiple people to stop and stare as he ran down the alley that led to the fields. He started to slow down as his age and poor diet caught up with him and he had to stop and catch his breath. Had he looked behind him at any point he would have noticed the clown start to follow him and would have noticed her watching him now as he stood up and walked around the hill to the ruins of the cottage where he started to dig through looking for the tunnel. She decided not to make herself known just yet instead waiting until he broke through.

It took him a while to get to the bottom of the rubble considering he was doing it himself, but he didn't know how to access the staircase and was still too panicked from seeing the clown to think of anything smarter. Eventually he got down to the hole but couldn't move the support beam on top of it so instead opted to push it as far as he could to one side and try to squeeze down the gap he created. It was getting slightly claustrophobic considering how big he was, and he started to wonder why it was him doing this chalice and not Penny.

Penny was making her way up to Abigail's house and trying to decipher the map on the way to figure out where the twins were hiding. Some people questioned what she was up to when she started approaching the mayor's house, but she showed them her police badge and that quelled any questions from most citizens. She decided it was smarter to enter from the back door since she didn't fully trust the hinges on the front door since she kicked it in last time.

As she entered the house, she had to watch her step as she navigated around the mess they had left from their previous exploits. Penny started to feel bad about how much trouble they had caused for the people in this town. She reassured herself in the belief that it was all for a good cause especially if Grail was telling the truth when he filled her in on the story of Danbrann.

She came to the door that led to the tower and started making her way down but suddenly heard a cracking sound. She stopped to try and listen out for any follow-up noises, but the next crack came with the stairs crumbling beneath her feet and sending her crashing into the basement. She pulled herself up knowing that she'd be safe as long as she got through the door to the crypt but before she got there the twins jumped down and blocked the entrance.

Grail made his way through the cave and got to the crypt but before he made it over to the chalice, he heard a voice from behind him calling his name. He turned around to see the clown once again, this time making direct eye contact with him and grinning as she held Daniel's dagger and pointed it directly at him.

Grail went to speak but his voice got caught in his throat, so he instead brandished Abigail's dagger and pointed it at the clown with his hand visibly shaking from the nerves.

The clown started to run at him but as he raised the knife to defend himself, she flipped around him and cut a hole into his coat dropping the cup filled with his elixir. She picked it up and ran to the other side of the room where she gave the cup to Daniel as he descended down the stairs.

"I didn't have you pegged as a coulrophobe Mr Grail." He said with a smug grin painted across his face. Grail wondered if he knew about his dreams, but his mental questions were answered as Daniel began arrogantly monologuing. "I only made her wear the make-up as a way to blend in and spy on you must have sussed it out as you came running right over here. It's a shame really since I had just figured out that when you control an elder you can invite them into your crypt. I was desperate to see what an elixir with multiple doses of elder blood would do." As he spoke Grail was thinking at a million miles an hour trying desperately to think of a way out. It was obvious that Daniel didn't know about his dreams so why did they matter? Could they be the answer to ending this?

That's when he figured it out, Cliff said that the previous detectives went insane, the dreams were warnings, the village was messing with his mind. He was mortal; he wasn't supposed to be there. But every time the clown got involved in his dreams everything went black. Daniel just said that he was working on an elixir though, so Grail looked at the chalice and saw all the necessary ingredients inside. All that was left was the blood. With that he brandished the dagger one more time and sliced his hand open, pouring blood into the chalice and severing Daniel's immortality.

He recoiled from the pain, but the clown seemed to be stumbling too as she regained her free will, she turned to Daniel and drove the dagger into his neck killing him instantly. Finally, she raised her hands to her face and wiped off the make-up to reveal that the clown was Abigail being controlled by Daniel. There wasn't any time to ruminate on this however as the crypt started shaking and crumbling with it's master dead. So, Grail and Abigail both ran for the staircase.

Penny stood face to face with the twins and tried to think of a way to get them away from the door. They both took a fighting stance and had expressions of quiet confidence. Penny really didn't like fighting and certainly didn't want to fight any children, but she was far from helpless having to pass numerous physical trials to become a ranking police officer. She knew she could fight, and she could justify it to herself as well considering that the twins are almost definitely way older than her. The twins jumped at her and began raining punches while, to start with, Penny mostly played defensive whilst questioning them.

"Why do you even want to kill everyone?" She asked.

"Eternal life was a gift given to us when our mother invaded this village." Jasmine began.

"Everyone else stole it and must die for their transgressions." Added Jackson.

Penny was taken back by this; she hadn't really considered who the twin's parents were but if they're immortals it stands to reason that they'd have been around since before the village. She began to speak to try and reason with them and maybe even convince them to work alongside her in removing the immortality from the rest of the village, but she was interrupted as they already knew what she was going to suggest.

"You'd have to remove everyone's, including ours." Jasmine intercepted.

"The only way to get what we want is to kill." Jackson finished.

Now knowing for a fact that collaboration wasn't an option, Penny thought back to when she had fought the twins with Veronica before and how Jackson seemed somewhat protective of Jasmine and so Penny targeted her. With Penny sweeping Jasmine's legs and using her as a human shield, Jackson stopped fighting to avoid hitting his sister. Penny manoeuvred around him and pushed Jasmine into Jackson when her back was against the door then ran into the crypt where she knew they couldn't follow. She walked up to the chalice as the twins fought amongst themselves, Jasmine angry at Jackson for not stopping Penny and Jackson angry at Jasmine for letting Penny use her like that.

Penny pulled out the cup that Grail was given by Daniel and poured his elixir into the chalice severing Abigail's immortality. As she did, the crypt began to shake and collapse around her, she ran for the exit, but the twins noticed the crypt collapsing as well and stopped arguing long enough to close the door and prevent her from escaping as the entire place crashed on top of her.

Grail and Abigail made it out of Daniel's crypt just in time as it fell to pieces and they both stood up watching each other cautiously, they both slowly pulled their daggers out and Abigail went to attack Grail but she suddenly felt a strange feeling in her stomach and her face dropped as she realised that she's not immortal anymore as Grail ran up and plunged the dagger into her chest, taking the elixir cup from her as she fell.

He made his way back to the pub trying his best to remain as unseen as possible considering that he was covered in blood but when he got back he saw that Penny hadn't arrived yet, Veronica was pacing behind the bar and trying to serve as many customers as she could until she noticed

Grail and led him down to the basement, she asked how his mission went so he filled her in on all the details and Veronica breathed a sigh of relief since he was successful, he still had enough elixir for the twins, and the mayor dying was evidence that Penny was successful too.

Chapter 13

The Finale

Hours had passed since Grail had returned and both he and Veronica were growing increasingly concerned about Penny not having come back in all that time. Grail had disposed of his coat since it had a hole cut into it and was trying to scrub the blood out of his shirt in the basement while Veronica served customers in the pub and Cliff continued to rest in the inn as his age and newfound mortality crept up on him.

It had taken hours to dig through the rubble, get down the tower without any stairs and even just to get into Abigail's house. But Maurice was much more perceptive than the detectives had given him credit for and after watching their strange activity he figured out that something had to be going on with Abigail, especially since Penny had disappeared into her house hours ago and hadn't come out yet. She had shown him her badge when he questioned her earlier and he pretended to accept that as an appropriate answer but seeing the state of the inside of Abigail's house confirmed his suspicions.

He lifted the door no longer attached to the door frame off Penny and picked her up to carry her out. He had to hold her over his shoulder as he climbed the rope that he had tied to get out of the tower and then told passers-by that she had been drinking a bit too much when they asked what he was doing while he brought her back to his cafe and let her rest behind the counter.

Veronica ran down to see Grail finishing up cleaning his shirt and frantically told him that she just received a call from Maurice and that he said Penny was going to be okay. Grail donned his mask again and ran to the cafe where he saw Penny just starting to wake up. He thought that she would need a while to recover and was willing to find the twin's chalice alone, but she just rubbed her neck from the pain and asked Maurice to get her a black coffee.

Grail and Penny followed the map to the top of the mountain that stood above the village, they came to a cathedral overlooking the mountain range that secludes the village and each took a door to push it open. They came to an enormous open room with a giant statue of an angelic depiction of Danbrann at the far side of a staircase leading to some catacombs beneath the mountain. They wondered how such an impressive structure could be so well hidden within the mountains that they hadn't seen it from the village but shook it off as they descended into the catacombs.

As they reached the bottom of the stairs, they came to a long corridor with sarcophagi lining the walls, they slowly made their way down the unusually long corridor and finally came to a door like the one at the bottom of the tower in the mayor's house. What really grabbed their attention however was what was above the door. They saw Edith with blood dripping down the wall and door as she hung as if crucified against the wall. But she wasn't dead, and she would stay that way until Grail and Penny destroyed the immortality of the village.

They realised this and looked at each other unsure of what to do, she had lost too much blood by now to be saved without the magic, but they needed to stop the twins from killing the rest of the village, but could they be the ones responsible for an innocent old woman's death?

"It's the lesser of the evils, you know." Edith started to speak, straining her voice as she grew tired. "I've lived a long life. Unnaturally so. I couldn't ask you to stand by while evil was committed for my sake. Even if I did somewhat nurture it." She said solemnly as she drifted back to sleep before the detectives had a chance to respond. They each took a deep breath and Penny wiped a tear from her eye as they opened the door and stepped into the final crypt.

The two of them stepped into the crypt each holding one of the daggers and stood face to face with the twins who brandished their own daggers as they waited for the detectives to arrive. The twins split up and slowly circled around the detectives until Grail made the first move and lunged for the chalice. Jasmine jumped to intercept him, and Penny ran toward the right side of the room where Jackson was. She swung the dagger up across his shoulder, but he jumped back to avoid it cutting too deep and then ducked down and swiped his dagger across Penny's leg making her stumble, she caught herself and swung the dagger outwards as she turned herself back around to face Jackson.

Jasmine drove her dagger into Grail's left arm and pushed him away from the chalice, he grabbed her wrist and held the dagger in place to wrench it away from her, she stepped back and glared at him as his left arm went limp with the dagger still sticking out of it. With his right hand still holding his dagger he smirked knowing that he now had the upper hand since she was disarmed, regardless of how many actual arms either of them could utilise right now.

Penny swung at Jackson making him jump back and then she ran the other way giving her some distance between them as she circled around the room and aimed for Jasmine's back. Jackson chased after her and called out to Jasmine to watch out, that distracted her for long enough to give Grail the chance to charge her and plunge the dagger into her stomach as he tackled her to the ground. Penny jumped over them using Grail's right shoulder as a springboard and then as Jackson caught up Grail pulled the other knife out of his shoulder and they both stabbed each other's stomach. The twins stood up and removed the daggers.

"Did you forget that we're immortal?" Jasmine pointed out.

"No, I just had to keep you away from her." Grail responded as he clutched his stomach and gestured to Penny as she poured the elixir into the chalice, severing the entire village's immortality. As the final crypt came crashing around them Penny put Grail's arm around her shoulders and helped him get back out the way they came while the twins took a hidden staircase like Daniel had and made it out alive to possibly strike again someday.

An entire week had passed since the villagers had lost their immortality, of course for most of them, they noticed no difference, having lived blissfully unaware of their own power. But for some, life had changed dramatically, for example, without the mayor, the town had to have a new election and the local tailor seemed to be desperate for a change in career paths, his first act as new mayor was to hire a new sheriff as Penny had quit the police force.

Veronica finished filling in a grave and hugged Penny for comfort as they looked at the two tombstones laid out for Edith and Cliff. Grail walked up the hill to meet them, having visited the cafe on his way to pick up a coffee with plenty of cream and sugar.

"So those dreams have stopped completely now?" Asked Penny as she saw Grail approaching.

"Yeah, it seems it's really all over now. Although I never figured out what that little girl represented." He added thoughtfully.

"Maybe it's a new case?" Suggested Penny excitedly.

"If it is, I'll probably need your help, if you're up for it." Grail wondered. Penny grinned and nodded enthusiastically in response before turning to Veronica.

"What about you?" She asked with a touch of concern to her voice.

"I've still got my pub to run over here, but you guys are over in Sakkacity right? I think I'll have to swing by and see what it's like sometime." She answered with a confident smile before heading back to the bar and leaving the two detectives to find their way back. Grail started heading toward the road that he had walked down when he first came to the village but turned to see Penny standing there and staring into the town.

"You coming, partner?" He asked loud enough to snap her out of her trance. She smiled and nodded one more time before they left to find their next adventure.

Printed in Great Britain
by Amazon

79752314R00058